With an updated membership card to the Bad Girl's Club, the poems of *Enter Here* speed through highways of larceny and lust but cannot erase the roadkill from their rear-view mirrors. There is no promised land here: only a Didion-infused metropolis in which Los Angeles spreads out like a botched autopsy. An emotional tote board tallies love lost, love denied, no love but sex, sex as sport, and sex as redemption to chart the perilous course of single life on hard streets. Abandon all hope, ye ask? No room for error is offered. Instead, these poems give you seconds to decide on the one choice that might get you home safe. Prepare to savor a whirlwind of a ride. And it *is* quite a ride.

—Laurel Ann Bogen, poet and author of 11 books, including *The Last Girl in the Land of the Butterflies* and *Psychosis in the Produce Department: New and Selected Poems 1975-2015*

Not only does Alexis Rhone Fancher deliver the goods, she lets us roll underneath the sheet with her. Of all the languages one can master, Alexis speaks "chick" better than anyone I know. "This Mata Hari likes to watch," she says of her sister. Can a single poem capture the devastating effects of teenage adolescence and sibling rivalry in one fell swoop? It most certainly can.

This salacious poetry collection takes you from the desert all the way to the Hollywood Hills. "The two men stared at me the way my stepfather did." Alexis lays it all out like a chenille bedspread. "'*You're my first,*' I whisper, just to fuck with him," issuing a comedic sense of timing within ten sparse words. Mixing heartbreak and hilarity, these poems deliver an emotional wallop with the ease of a woman rolling down her nylons. Welcome to Los Angeles.

—Pam Ward, author of *Want Some Get Some* and *Bad Girls Burn Slow*

These poems are so erotic that even a perusal of their titles in a Table of Contents can evince an almost criminal arousal. But not to be overlooked is that their creator Alexis Rhone Fancher deals with all seven stages of human development, with an especially acute excursion into memories of adolescence. Alexis is not merely a detailed chronicler of our socio-physical interactions— she is by far the most exciting, articulate, and convincing storyteller in contemporary verse. Don't miss a single phrase, let alone an intimate scene.

—Gerald Locklin, prolific poet and fiction author whose 100+ books include *Poets and Pleasure Seekers, Children of a Lesser Demagogue, The Case of the Missing Blue Volkswagen,* and *The Death of Jean-Paul Sartre and Other Poems*

Enter Here is more than a diversion—it's a gift. When you enter these poems, you find a world where the borders between reality and dream sometimes blur; a world where the voice of the speaker is so clear and seductive that you can't stop reading; a world where love and sex and death, those universal themes, are made new by images so compelling that every poem, not just those accompanied by photographs, becomes a visual testament to the richness and complexity of a life fully lived. Alexis Rhone Fancher is as fearless as she is fierce, as unabashed as she is tender, and no one who enters here will leave unchanged by the power of her poems.

—Lynne Knight, author of *The Persistence of Longing*

Enter Here reminds me of being twelve and finding my father's *Penthouses* in the bottom of his closet—except these poems are honest and raw, lurid and luscious, brave. They strut across the page with the steadily simmering narratives of a master storyteller composed of clean, tight lines stacked with startling images and a language that sings in your skin. With a well thought-out arc and strong poems that stand on their own but get even bigger brushing up against each other, this book is poignant, powerful, and stays with you. Buy it—plain brown wrapper optional.

—Tony Gloeggler, author of *Until the Last Light Leaves, The Last Lie,* and *One Wish Left*

Any self-styled critic who characterizes Alexis Rhone Fancher's written work as only sexy stanzas would be making an egregious mistake. Far more accurate to portray her poetry as grainy, gritty, noir images by a female version of Henry Miller's bitter observation of the dirty word "relationships," or Georges Bataille's eccentric business of the creative woman at times catering to the psycho-sado fantasies of her lover, or Stephen Schneck's nightmare world of sensual dreams, but with an added dose of infectious humor. Alexis Rhone Fancher's words are cartwheels churning through the too often misunderstood, labyrinthine sandbox of erotica.

—Michael C. Ford, music journalist, playwright, Grammy-nominated spoken-word artist (*Language Commando)*, and Pulitzer Prize-nominated poet (*Emergency Exits)*

ENTER HERE

poems by

alexis rhone fancher

Enter Here
poems by
alexis rhone fancher

ISBN: 978-0-9862703-7-6

First edition: May 2017

Published by KYSO Flash Press: www.kysoflash.com
Seattle, Washington, USA. Printed in the USA.

All poems and photographs published herein are copyrighted by
Alexis Rhone Fancher. All rights reserved.

This book was designed and produced by Clare MacQueen, in
collaboration with Alexis Rhone Fancher.

Poems are reprinted here from numerous journals and magazines.
Please see Acknowledgments for details.

Except for short quotations within critical articles or reviews, no
portion of this book, including its covers, may be used,
reproduced, or transmitted in any form or by any means, electronic
or mechanical, including photocopying and recording, or by any
information storage or retrieval system, without permission in
writing from the Author.

Please send questions and comments to:

Author: alexis@lapoetrix.com

Publisher: KYSOWebmaster@gmail.com

Also by Alexis Rhone Fancher:

State of Grace: The Joshua Elegies

How I Lost My Virginity to Michael Cohen
and other heart-stab poems

For Fancher

Table of Contents

17 When I turned fourteen, my mother's sister took me to lunch and said:

18 Daddy's Friend, Stan

20 When I turned sixteen, Mother let Uncle Kenny from Chicago take me for a ride

23 Family Tree

25 Spreading My Legs for Someone (Posing for Pirelli)

27 Double Date: The Quarterback, the Fullback, & the High Cost of Dinner

29 Tuesday Nights, Room 28 of the Royal Motel on Little Santa Monica

31 Tattooed Girl in a Sheer, White Blouse (Sushi Bar Fantasy)

33 Tatooed Girl on the Roof of King Eddy's Saloon with a Run in Her Last Pair of Stockings

35 the cool wind comes through me like Jamaica

37 Freeway Sex

38 Tonight I Dream of Anjelica, My First Ex-Girlfriend, Who Taught Me the Rules of the Road...

39 When your mother convinces you to take in your homeless younger sister

41 Norwegian Wood *(A cento love poem composed entirely of text from Haruki Murakami's 1987 novel by the same name)*

43 Boy Toy (Learning to Share)

44 For the Sad Waitress at the Diner in Barstow

46 Bambi Explains It All

48 Stiletto Killer...a Surmise

50 Three Little Words

52 Doggy-Style Christmas

53 Tonight I Dream of My First True Love (*Ménage à Trois*)

54 Larceny: A Story in Eleven Parts *(18-Year-Olds Victoria and Debi Flee Los Angeles in Debi's Blue Toyota Camry, and Take the Pacific Coast Highway North with Only a Smattering of Stars to Light Their Way...)*

57 To my new boyfriend with oversized blue lips tattooed on his neck

59 Tatooed Girl: Slice/Shokunin

60 Play It As It Lays *(A cento composed entirely of text from Joan Didion's 1970 novel)*

62 Years & Years Later I Am Still Not That Girl, Laughing

64 June Fairchild isn't dead—

66 Tonight I Dream of My Last Meal with My First Ex-Husband, Who Was Both Fickle and Bent

67 Tonight I Dream of My Second Ex-Husband, Who Played Piano Better than Herbie Hand-Cock

68 Out of Body

69 Because He Used to Love Her: A Story in Photographs & Senryu

74 Regarding the Unreliability of Buses in the Desert in Late July

76 For Lynnie in the Dark

78 When the Handsome, Overgrown Samoan Boy Stands Again in Front of Your Glass-Walled Beach House in Venice & Begins to Masturbate, Never Taking His Eyes Off You...

79 I Was Hovering Just Below the Hospital Ceiling, Contemplating My Death

81 Five Ways I'm a Bad Girl

82 At Eighteen

83 Red-Handed in Canoga Park: How Everything Is All My Fault

84 Morning Wood

85 Housekeeping

86	Tonight We Will Bloom for One Night Only
87	Roman Holiday
88	I Prefer Pussy (a little city-kitty ditty)
89	Cousin Elaine from Chicago and I Are Naked
91	Dear Mrs. Brown, Your Husband Whimpers When He Comes...
93	Last Dance in NoHo
95	Daylight Savings Won't Save Us
96	Snow White: For Desirée, Former Headliner at 4Play Gentlemen's Club
98	For Kate in Absentia
100	this small rain
103	Acknowledgments: Photographs
104	Acknowledgments: Previous Publications by Title of Poem
107	Acknowledgments: Previous Publications by Title of Venue
110	Author's Bio
111	Author's Self-Portrait
112	Author's Note

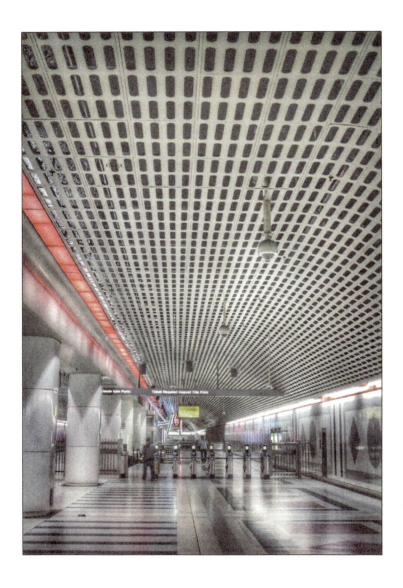

When I turned fourteen, my mother's sister took me to lunch and said:

soon you'll have breasts. They'll mushroom
on your smooth chest like land mines.

A boy will show up, a schoolmate, or the gardener's son.
Pole-cat around you. All brown-eyed persistence.

He'll be everything your parents hate, a smart aleck,
a dropout, a street racer on the midnight prowl.

Even your best friend will call him a loser.
But this boy will steal your reason, have you

writing his name inside a scarlet heart, entwined
with misplaced passion and a bungled first kiss.

He'll bivouac beneath your window, sweet-talk you
until you sneak out into his waiting complications.

Go ahead, tempt him with your new-found glamour.
Tumble into the back seat of his Ford at the top of Mulholland,

flushed with stardust, his mouth in a death-clamp on your nipple,
his worshipful fingers scatting sacraments on your clit.

Soon he will deceive you with your younger sister,
the girl who once loved you most in the world.

Daddy's Friend, Stan

1.
Stan likes me in those cut-off jeans that fringe
my upper thighs, fringe I unravel when I watch
TV, after my homework's done.

I do it for Stan.

2.
He says I'm rocking this silver
bikini. It makes my nipples hard.

3.
He says in this suit I look like "moonlight
flickering in a jar."

4.
Swimming laps.
Going nowhere. Disastrous
pair: Daddy's flirty little girl, and his
good friend, Stan. Beer in hand. Watching
when he thinks no one's watching.

I swim for Stan.

5.
Smolder-eyed, half-lidded, snake.

6.
He almost touched me.
He never touched me.
He almost never touched me:

Choose one.

7.
Driving me home
from Northridge, Stan's daughter Ruthie
asleep in back; me, strapped
in front, the seatbelt dissecting
my budding breasts.

Stan's speeding,
his eyes on the road,
left hand on the wheel,
right hand lost in the no-man's land
between my knees and thighs.
"Shhh!" he soothes when I whimper,
afraid he's gone too far.

He thumbs the fabric instead of me,
whistles the theme from
Mission Impossible.

That fringe! That fringe! Oh, that fringe!

When I turned sixteen, Mother let Uncle Kenny from Chicago take me for a ride

1.
Uncle Kenny let the top down on the Chrysler,
fedora protecting his tender scalp.

When I got into the car
he threw his arm over the bucket seat,
fingers grazing the back of my skimpy tube top.

2.
PCH, left on Sunset, he took Deadman's Curve
like a pro, then the slow cruise
to downtown. Like he'd been here before.

July baked my bare shoulders.
Like Uncle Kenny, I burned easily.

3.
Sunset ended at Olivera Street.
My uncle chose La Golondrina Cafe.
I ordered the cheese enchiladas.
He ordered a double Margarita, extra salt.

Things I Learned At Lunch:
Dress Well.
Travel Light.
Marry Up.

My mom says you're good for nothing, I said.

Uncle Kenny slid so close in the booth
his trousers tickled my thigh.

I once made love to Hedy Lamarr,
he confessed.

He ran his tongue around the rim
of the margarita glass, licked the salt.
His blue eyes stared right past me.

When the mariachis reached
our table, Uncle Kenny pulled me from the booth,
spun me around the restaurant.

Like all big men, he was light on his feet.

4.
The overpriced gold and ruby chandelier earrings
serenaded us from the store window.

5.
How much damage, my mother reasoned,
can he do my girl in one afternoon?

6.
When Uncle Kenny died soon after
in flagrante delicto, no one was surprised.

I heard it was his heart, my mother said,
but I know he didn't have one.

She clipped his obituary out of the paper,
pinned it to the refrigerator with a magnet.

In *my* heart I knew differently.

I drove PCH north, left on Sunset,
an Uncle Kennyesque fedora
shading my eyes.

At Dead Man's Curve
I threw my head back like I'd seen
Hedy Lamarr do in the movies.

My chandelier earrings tinkled in the wind.

Family Tree

My younger sister
climbs my limbs, steals my clothes,

sleeps at the foot of my bed,
calls it worship.

She wants the gold locket between
my breasts. She wants my breasts.

She wants my life.
It's been crowded since the day she arrived.

The slut who is my younger sister
shinnies up my tree, clambers my branches,

straddles my limbs.

She inserts herself into my conversations,
seduces my best friend,

eats my dessert.

This Mata Hari likes to watch,

(his tongue down my throat
hand up my skirt in the bedroom),

spills to our parents my every sin,
calls it reverence.

And my first love?
She covets him, too.

One day she'll chop me down
to reach him.

Spreading My Legs for Someone (Posing for Pirelli)

The grey-suited Pirelli rep sat behind the desk,
puffing on a cigarette. White smoke hung in the air
like surrender.

I slipped off my dress.
Kept my stilettos.

There was nothing on the agency man's glass-topped
brain but my nakedness.
He wouldn't meet my eye.

"*Jesus!*" he exclaimed when I bent over
to tighten an ankle strap.

The photographer looked like Antonio Banderas.
"Sit down on the seamless," he said, pointing
to the black backdrop that spilled onto the floor.

He rolled the tire over to me, snapped on the lights.
I sat, cross-legged, clutching the tire close.

My naked breasts peeked through the center,
the nipples erect. I laid my hot face along the tread.

The photographer pushed up his cashmere sleeves,
picked up his Nikon.

The lights bore down like August; the cement
below the seamless bruised my ass. The two men
stared at me the way my stepfather did.

I pushed the damp strands of hair from my forehead.
Arched my back. Opened my thighs.

The suit lit another cigarette.
Antonio Banderas moved in for a close-up.

"Is this what you want?" I asked.

My feet poked out from the tire's rubber frame
like destiny.

Double Date: The Quarterback, the Fullback, & the High Cost of Dinner

When the night ends, your sister will
kiss the fullback goodnight on tiptoe,
under the porch light, her soft curls a halo
illuminating her naivety.

You, on the other hand,
will stare at your bare feet.
Not shy: Sullied. Seething.

Your sister will thank the fullback for dinner
at Tony's on the Pier,
the copious cocktails and signature chocolate mousse.
She'll tell him she had a wonderful time.
That she hopes she'll see him again.

You will say none of these things.
You will mind your manners.
You will try not to think how the quarterback
forced himself into your mouth.

You will bite your tongue and smile,
pretend his baller body
hasn't just slammed into yours,
that he didn't wipe his penis on your sheets
when he was done,

that while he was assaulting you,
you didn't wonder if the fullback was out there,
raping your sister. If he, too, was brutal.

In fact, your sister and the fullback only
watched TV, making out, but just a little.

You had no way to know this.

You lay there and took it for your sister.
You thought about her delicate spine,
believing if you played it wrong,
he might snap her like a sparrow.

They eyed the closed door of your bedroom.
They shared a knowing smile.
They knew nothing.

Tuesday Nights, Room 28 of the Royal Motel on Little Santa Monica

John Colton likes to call me *sweet girl.*
He likes to call me *baby cakes.*
He likes to call me late at night,
after his wife's asleep.

Tuesday nights at the Royal Motel
I vamp for him in the steamed-up bathroom.

He likes to watch me shave
my legs in the tub.
He likes to shave my bush
into a valentine.

He likes to watch me
pinch my nipples till his dick gets hard,
then push my pudenda
into his wet smile.

Tuesday nights at the Royal Motel
John Colton says it's better with me on top.
I ride him slo-mo, adagio.
First gear.

I could be anyone.
A Maserati, a long-lost symphony,
a one-time spritz at the fragrance counter
at Sak's Fifth Avenue.

He could be my father.

Tuesday nights at the Royal Motel
John Colton lights my Marlboro
after we fuck.

We watch the match burn down
to his fingertips.

I'm afraid to blow it out.

Tuesday nights at the Royal Motel
he holds me like I matter.

It's just sex, he sighs.
He brushes the hair from my face,
plants a kiss on my forehead.

You're my first, I whisper,
just to fuck with him.

Tuesday night at the Royal Motel
when John Colton doesn't show
I wait by the side of the bed.

In the morning, the voice mail.
The fire. The accidental burning.

I burn for you, sweet girl, he said.

Tattooed Girl in a Sheer, White Blouse
(Sushi Bar Fantasy)

1. In the Restaurant

I want to unbutton her. I need to run
my fingers down her rainbow skin,
expose the peekaboo of her sleeves.
I have a suspicion what's underneath:
the clouds, the python, the sloe-eyed siren
who clings to the cliff of her narrow hips,
the hyacinths behind her knees.
I want to see for myself.

2. In the Ladies'

She's washing herself in the sink like
Madonna's desperate Susan: neck, armpits,
breasts. Lucky me.
She asks me to scrub her back;
I trace a lotus flower atop indigo waves,
the springboard for a hummingbird with
iridescent wings. I dream about such things.

She aims the hand dryer on the wall at her
throat, lifts her arms above her head. On her
right bicep, a Kyoto dragon wrestles with
the sun; on her left, the beginnings of a crescent moon,
a festoon of stars twinkling on her wrists like
diamond tennis bracelets.

3. Indiscretion

She unbuttons her jeans,
shimmies them down around her ankles.
Above her mons a red heart ripped asunder,

and something written in Japanese.
"What does it say?"
"Whatever you want it to."
I want it to say "Enter Here."

4. In My Heart

See our reflections in the mirror
above the sink,
me, looking worshipful, ravenous.
She looks like the girl who'll choose
the tattoo needle over me, romance it until
there's nothing left for wounding.

I should have found her sooner.

Tattooed Girl on the Roof of King Eddy's Saloon with a Run in Her Last Pair of Stockings

L.A. spreads out below me like an autopsy.

I unhook the garters, roll the stockings down
my legs like used condoms.

When I bend over,
the Santa Ana wind licks my thighs, tears
at my panties, makes me moan like
he once did. I warned him I'd be in the wind;
no one holds me for long.

To hold me he'd have to kill me.

Inside King Eddy's, the regulars hemorrhage cash
for a jigger, eviscerate themselves
for a smile.

Chet Baker sings on the juke box with his broken
life, but nobody's dancing.

Everyone's gone searching for the "tattooed girl."
The bastard's offered a reward.
They're looking under tables, behind the bar, along
the Desperation aisle of the Last Bookstore.

I catch a glint of steel.

"Go ahead! Aim the revolver at my
heart. It's where I'm least vulnerable."

He wants me to jump. Save him a bullet.

And tonight I think, *Why not?*
When the key-light moon finds me,
when the Santa Anas roil the gathering crowd,
whip the black of my hair, push me to the edge,
I put up no struggle.

I hold the ruined stockings so they fill with wind.
Watch them tarantella away from my hands.

the cool wind comes through me like Jamaica

—for T.M.

outside, it's winter.
your life calls.

your wife calls.

you want to sail away.

turn back!

travel instead my aestival coastline,
throat,
collarbone,
my perfect breasts
sloped like berms in December.

brave the Bermuda Triangle
of my hips
and my belly,

the delectable delta
between my thighs;

plunder those places
your wife won't
let you go.

desire rules our ocean.
your body echoes my
perfume.

if she loved you as I do,
you wouldn't be here.

I wouldn't taste like you.

Enter Here | 36

Freeway Sex

There's a 19-car pileup on Vasquez Rocks.
You're late. This would be a good excuse.

I want to grind that thought out like your cigarette.
Drive right over it.

You were dead to me the first time
I found motel matches
in your pocket.

You brought me off-ramp roses.
Your fingers smelled like someone else.

When the traffic doesn't move,
when I'm lost again in Pasadena
and my pussy dampens,
I think of fellating you on the freeway
to pass the time.

Is that what you're thinking of?

From the 5 to the 2 to the 134.
Take the Pearblossom Highway.
Make a smooth transition.

Tell me exactly how it's going down and
I'll write that poem.

The one where you're supposed to be
on time, and I'm supposed to care.

Tonight I Dream of Anjelica, My First Ex-Girlfriend, Who Taught Me the Rules of the Road...

Anjelica comes on to me like a man, all slim-hipped swagger, relentless, dangling that red, '57 T-Bird at me like dessert. *Lemme take you for a ride, chica,* she sez after acting class. I figure what's the harm, but Ms. Angel Food gets out of hand. I don't count on her heart-shaped ass, or those brown nipples crammed in my mouth. I don't count on the Dial-O-Matic four-way, power leather seats, the telescoping steering wheel, or the frantic pleasure of her face between my thighs. I admit, I've always been driven to sin. But Anjelica's far from blameless. She rides me hard, week after week, double clutches me into ecstasy, hipbone against hipbone, the dulcet, lingering groan of our gears, grinding. When I confess the affair to my boyfriend, he jacks himself off in the galley kitchen, comes all over his unattainable fantasies. He says he doesn't consider sex between women to be cheating, and begs me to set up a threesome. I tell him the T-Bird's a two-seater, and watch his face fall. I could end it, but why? All I can say is, I want her for myself. All I can say is, I'm a die-hard romantic. Anyone I do, I do for love.

When your mother convinces you to take in your homeless younger sister

She will date your boyfriend.
She'll do it better than you ever did.
She'll have nothing but time.
He'll start showing up when you leave,
train her to make him the perfect BLT
(crusts off, avocado on the side),
encourage his cheating heart,
suck his dick so good he'll think
he's died and gone to Jesus.

Your sister will borrow your clothes,
and look better in them than you ever did.
Someone will see her with your boyfriend
at the Grove, agonize for days
before deciding not to tell you.
Meanwhile he'll buy her that fedora
you admired in Nordstrom's window, the last one
in your size.

When you complain, your mother
will tell you it's about time you learned to share.

While you're at work, your sister will tend your garden,
weed the daisies, coax your gardenias into bloom.
No matter how many times you remind her,
she will one day forget to lock the gate;
your cat and your lawn chairs will disappear.

Your mother will say it serves you right.

Your sister will move into your boyfriend's
big house in Laurel Canyon. He will ignore her,

and she will make a half-hearted suicide attempt;
you'll rescue her once again.

Your mother will wash her hands of the pair of you,
then get cancer and die.

Smell the white gardenias in the yard.
Cherish their heady perfume. Float them in a crystal bowl.
Forgive your sister as she has forgiven you.

Norwegian Wood

(A cento love poem composed entirely of text from Haruki Murakami's 1987 novel by the same name)

1.
It rained on her birthday.

2.
I could feel the soft swell of her breasts on my chest.

She herself had become small and narrow.
Don't worry, I said. *Just relax.*

Before I knew it, I was kissing her.

Her breathing intensified and her throat began to tremble.
I parted her long, slim legs.

But I'm scared, she said.

She seemed to be turning over something in her mind.

Do you have a girl you like? she asked.

I took a sip of wine, as if I had never heard anything.

3.
We were alive, she and I.

I moved my lips up her neck to her ear and took a nipple
with the finger of my other hand.

We explored each other's bodies in the darkness without words.

It was easy. Almost too easy.

4.
Glass shattered somewhere.
I felt no pain to speak of, but the blood wouldn't stop.

5.
I smelled the meadow grass, heard the rain at night.

6.
It was easy to tell which room was hers.
All I had to do was find the one window toward the back
where a faint light trembled.

Come in, she said.

Boy Toy (Learning to Share)

I stood in the doorway and watched Davy fuck my sister by candlelight (he never fucked me by candlelight). Their shadows conjoined, elegant. I was touching myself under my robe when they saw me. Two against one, I turned down the hall, turned down a threesome again. I'd brought him home because he talked like Davy Jones. I'd always wanted to fuck Davy Jones. So I let him be British all over me. An Anglophile, my roommate younger sister blossomed like a petunia. I thought I was learning to share. But that last night, when the sirens raged and the dogs howled in the dark, when love had me (suddenly) by the throat and my sister swore she could take him or leave him, how could I ever believe her? Anything I wanted, she wanted. So when he ping-ponged between her bed and mine, I told Davy to wear a condom. I told him I didn't know where she'd been. And when I finally begged Davy to make a choice, I watched his face carefully, ignored the implications of his sigh. *She's beautiful, your sister,* Davy said as he stroked my thigh.

For the Sad Waitress at the Diner in Barstow

beyond the kitchen's swinging door,
beyond the order wheel and the pass-through piled
high with bacon, hash browns, biscuits and gravy,

past the radio, tuned to 101.5 FM,
All Country—All the Time,
past the truckers overwhelming the counter,
all grab-ass and longing,

in the middle of morning rush
you'll catch her, in a wilted pink uniform,
coffee pot fused in her grip, staring over
the top of your head.

you'll follow her gaze, out the fly-specked, plate
glass windows, past the parking lot,

watch as she eyes those 18-wheelers barreling
down the highway, their mud guards
adorned with chrome silhouettes of naked women
who look nothing like her.

the cruel sun throws her inertia in her face.
this is what regret looks like.

maybe she's searching for that hot day in August
when she first walked away from you.

there's a choking sound
a semi makes, when it pulls off
the highway; that downshift a death rattle
she's never gotten used to.

maybe she's looking for a way back.
maybe she's ready to come home.

(but for now) she's lost herself
between the register and the door, the endless
business from table to kitchen;

she's as much leftover as those sunny-side eggs,
yolks hardening on your plate.

Bambi Explains It All

When I ask about living
in pockets of squalor,
Bambi explains it, says
it's a matter of stare
straight ahead, navigate
the gutters and don't
wear any good jewelry.

I've seen her svelte self
on Spring Street,
a determined click clack
of four-inch heels, both thumbs
texting. I've hailed her
by name from yards away.
Perfectly aloof. No reaction.
Both eyes glued to the screen.

When I ask about walking
her dog after midnight,
Bambi explains it, says
she feels safe at 3 a.m.
(in a two-block radius), says
people with dogs have
disposable income, tend
to stay put.

When I ask about living
with her gay best friend,
Bambi explains it, says
their devouring passion
goes beyond the sexual. But
still, he brings men home.

I've seen her stand lost
in her kitchen, when she
thinks no one's looking;
I've seen the calm acceptance
in her eyes.

When I ask about singleness
in a cruel city,
Bambi explains it all, says
every ten years,
reinvent yourself.
Get a gay husband.
Stay lonely.
Buy a dog.

—for Bambi Here

Stiletto Killer...a Surmise

"She told me if anybody screwed with her they'd get a stiletto heel in the eye," her former apartment manager tells TV news.

Alf and Ana drank tequila at the club until closing.

Ana wore a tight, green dress. Alf said she looked like a whore.

Back at the apartment, the neighbors heard screams.

"The defense will prove she was a battered woman," her lawyer told the press.

She was too short when the stilettos came off but her feet ached.

She had to stand on tiptoe to reach him, for Christ's sake.

Women are always losers in Texas.

Ana alleged, *He cursed in Swedish when he beat me.*

She'd read Swedes beat their women, in *The Girl With The Dragon Tattoo.*

In the early morning hours, Ana stabbed her lover thirty-one times.

The stiletto heel fused to her fist.

When the police arrived Ana was covered in blood.

In that green dress she looked like Christmas.

Three Little Words

—for Francesca Bell

1.
M has never said *I love you* before.
Not to me.

2.
He cries at weddings, like a girl.

3.
The sex is only good if we're totally fucked up.
It blurs how wrong we are for each other.

4.
English is not M's native tongue. It eludes him.

5.
Maybe he misspoke?
His prepositions hang mid-air.

He says it's hard to think when it's hard.

6.
M's white teeth nibble at my clit like a ferret.
The two front ones indent slightly;
it makes him look goofy, like a joke.

Sometimes when we have sex, M's calico meow trips
across my back. Rakes a claw. Caterwauls.

She doesn't want me here.

Sometimes when we have sex, *I* am the one in heat.

7.
Outside, the tin-roof rain suicides
on the hard-packed earth.

M is fucking me from behind, his
body melded into my ass, fingers kneading my breasts.
He's mumbling up the courage.
I know what he's trying to say.
I want to fuck him mute.

8.
In the bedroom
a Dennis Hopper photo of Tuesday Weld,
driving, top down, blonde hair streaming.
Circa 1968. She's unfettered.

Why can't he see that
I am that girl, *my* top down,
my hair streaming,
my consequence-less life?

9.
M. bought the print for me but
I don't want it.
I want nothing from him but
a silent film, a carnival.
I want him to want that, too.

I want him to shut up but
he zeros in on my ear

and says it.

Doggy-Style Christmas

I saw your twin on Spring Street. He looked like Christmas. His Santa outfit, complete with full, white beard, furry red jacket, and black patent leather belt, was perfect. His belly looked like yours. Like you, he had a pit bull on a leash, but this one sported Petco antlers and the booties so common on these dirty, L.A. streets. A huge, red bell clanged from his spiked collar with each tail wag. When Santa crouched low to rearrange the antlers, his red jacket rode up, his elastic-waistband pants slid down, and I saw the words "Doggy Style" tramp-stamped across his lower back in four-inch, luridly colored, Gothic letters. It reminded me how much I missed you, how doggy style was our favorite position, the one where you achieved maximum penetration, I didn't have to look at you, and every day was Christmas.

Tonight I Dream of My First True Love (*Ménage à Trois*)

"Trembling, like Paris, on the brink
of an obscure and formidable revolution."
—Victor Hugo

It feels like a competition. I lie between the two of them, sweltering, like Paris in August. Gene's lanky six-foot-four-inches hang off the foot of the bed; Brett's dancer-body liquid, compact, is curled into mine, his hard need pressed against my thigh. I'm not sure how I ended up here, in love with a man who wants me to fuck his best friend while he watches. Now the three of us crowd in my too-small bed. I stare at a black and white photo of Montmartre on the ceiling. Brett trembles like a needle to the pole. Van Morrison's on the radio, having sex in the green grass with the brown-eyed girl. The ceiling fan rotates counterclockwise, but we're all sweating. I should have moved the beds together when my roommate moved out, but it's too late now that Gene's spread my thighs, and pinned his best friend against the wall; and he says nothing while Brett watches him slam into me. I need him to scream *I love you!* again and again like he did before. But Gene's eyes are locked with Brett's. I see what I'm not meant to see: I am disposable, nothing more than a deep hole. A hot rain pelts the bedroom window. Gene pours into me like runoff. His tears look like raindrops on glass. I turn his face so he can see what he is losing. I want him to watch his best friend as he arches his dancer's back and comes in my mouth, his spasms an arabesque. I pull back my hair and dip my head, *trembling, like Paris, on the brink of an obscure and formidable revolution.*

Larceny: A Story In Eleven Parts

*(18-Year-Olds Victoria and Debi Flee Los Angeles
in Debi's Blue Toyota Camry, and Take the Pacific Coast
Highway North with Only a Smattering of Stars
to Light Their Way...)*

1. Into The Dark
The night highway crawls with creatures. Moths headfirst into the windshield, lizards, mice, besotted by headlights, crushed flat beneath their tires. Sheltered, stupid, the girls pick up a stranger. Thinking this is his lucky day, longhaired Danny tumbles into the back seat.

2. Back Story
When Victoria moved in with Debi's family, junior year, her mom never realized she was missing. Now Victoria surveys her flawless skin, full lips, and thick blond hair in the rearview mirror; sees instead her mother's eyes, her dead daddy's smile.

3. Just Outside Of Pismo Beach: An Adventure!
Their route mirrors the shoreline. They speed to outdistance the past. Victoria tallies roadkill. It makes her think of her dad. When she tosses their purses in the back seat with Danny, he recalls the first time he snapped a cat's neck, but stops short of telling.

4. Luck Of The Draw
Debi's fingers run through her kinky black curls. She's ironed her hair into submission, endured the dryer, hair rolled large in rinsed, frozen orange-juice cans. Jagger struts out of the radio. Debi hums off-key.

5. Choices
If he has a choice, Danny'd go for the brunette. The blonde is hotter, but she looks like trouble. Somehow, trouble always finds

him. *Where you headed?* Victoria asks. Danny looks from one girl to the other. *Hell in a handbasket,* he grins.

6. The Low-Down
Debi wants Victoria's beauty. Victoria wants Debi's mom. Each dances in the other's cast-off, each glows in the dark. Danny susses their singular affection. He's a good observer, an only child. Danny wants only their wallets.

7. Night Swim
The Lorelei moon lures the trio off-course. Tempted, they exit the highway, strip down to their skivvies, hurl themselves into the sea. Danny revels in the half-naked beauties, cavorting just for him in the moonlight. Out of their depth, Debi's fingers accidentally brush Victoria's left breast. As they come together, breathless, past the breakers, the peace is almost unbearable.

8. Truth or Dare
Midnight confessions. Danny never finished high school. Victoria's afraid of men. Debi takes the dare. Climbs the retaining wall and howls like a lunatic. Better this than her secrets spilled. When the big wave washes over her, Debi stands her ground. When Danny grabs her anyway, she licks his face.

9. On The Road Again
Debi tends to dwell. Night driving clears her head. She chews a strand of her hair, sips vodka out of an Evian bottle. She misses Freddy's thick cock. Wonders why she ever left him. Approaching Morgan Hill, Debi finds a motel, reckons Danny owes her and Victoria for the ride.

10. Karma: The Condensed Version
It's the best day of Danny's life. In slumber, *he looks like baby Jesus,* Victoria sighs. Debi rescues their wallets from Danny's backpack. His, too. The North Star beckons. They'll make San

Francisco by morning. The motel air conditioner's rattle masks their departure.

11. The Last Leg

Victoria drives while Debi counts Danny's money. The Toyota eats up the highway, a rocket to their nascent future. She'll buy souvenirs in the city, maybe a gift for her mom. When Debi sticks her head out the window, even Victoria's chatter can't drown out the sound the wind makes.

To my new boyfriend with oversized blue lips tattooed on his neck

Is it your ex's pout? I wonder. Blue
and on your neck. Full lips, parted
like an invitation—

a visual love poem.

Daytime, I keep to your good side,
your skin unsullied.

But in the night while you sleep
I match my lips to the imprint

tongue the moue
of my predecessor's mouth,
lick her salty legacy,
and come up thin.

I can't sleep for wondering
if she's for real,

if she wore your pants,
mouthed your prayers,
sucked you off like a Hoover?

I want them to be some stranger's lips.
Clip art, a souvenir of a three-day bender
in the company of sailors.

Instead, after whisky and kinky sex,
one night you let it slip:

how just before she kissed you off
she led you on a leash,

sat you in the chair,
cupped your chin,

imprinted her lipsticked kiss on your
neck's throbbing pulse,

and ordered the tattooist to begin.

Tattooed Girl: Slice/Shokunin*

He wants to slice me, covets firm flesh,
promises a clean cut, carries his knives

with him, like luck in his pocket. He wants
to sway me, fillet me, serve me

with ponzu sauce, ginger,
a hot smear of wasabi. Says, *You won't feel a thing.*

He cuts the friends out of my life. Cuts
my family. My dog.

He cuts when no one's hungry and all
the patrons are gone.

He cuts my reticence razor thin,
cuts the refusal from my lips.

He cuts my pleasure with betrayal. Says,
Tell me it doesn't feel good.

Look, a single eyelash adorns the *nigiri.*
My DNA's all over it.

He was right. I didn't feel a thing.

---

* *Shokunin* means master craftsman and may also be used to refer to
sushi chef.

Play It As It Lays

"She was intent upon her reflection in the mirror behind the table,
tracing a line with one finger from her chin to her temple."
—from *Play It As It Lays* (Joan Didion, 1970)

(A cento composed entirely of text from Didion's novel)

1.
Pretty good, she heard herself say after only the slightest pause.

She felt nothing.
She tried to straighten a drawer, and abandoned it.
I missed a transition, he said finally.

2.
She had at last done something that reached him, but now
it was too late.

Some people resist, he said.
The water in the pool was always 85 degrees
and it was always clean.
Some people don't want to know.

3.
For days during the rain she did not speak out loud
or read a newspaper.

What am I supposed to do, he had said before he left the house.
I mean we could definitely stand a few giggles.

4.
A few days later the dreams began.

You're lying in water and it's warm and you hear
your mother's voice.
In the past few minutes he had significantly altered
her perception of reality.
She said that it was not too cold.

5.
It came with the rent.

What in fuck am I supposed to do?
His voice was measured, uninflected, as if he had been
saying the words to himself all night.

6.
She leaned against the padded elevator wall and closed her eyes.
How much do you want it, he used to say.

7.
Do you think he talked to God?
I mean do you think God answered?

Years & Years Later I Am Still Not That Girl, Laughing

—for Susan Hayden

Monday.
All that green-eyed sorrow
spilling out like a landslide.

Tuesday.
Inside our last time:

You looked my way.
I took off my shirt.
Pressed my tits against the glass.

Wednesday.
The snow ghosts schuss
in my dreams,

a dirge.

Thursday.
The phone rings.
The waitresses add up.

I sit on the counter, skirt hiked high,
like one of those girls who even now
keeps calling and calling.

Friday.
Too many people loved you.

Saturday.
I spend it not mourning you.

The way you avalanched
downhill into oblivion.

Oblivious.

Sunday.
"I don't know how you get up in the morning,"
you said to me after you died.

June Fairchild isn't dead—

she's planning a comeback.
she's snorting Ajax for the camera.
she's landing a role on *I Spy.*
she's writing her number on a napkin and
handing it to me at King Eddy's Saloon.

June Fairchild isn't dead—
she's just been voted Mardi Gras Girl at Aviation High.
she's acting in a movie with Roger Vadim.
she's gyrating at Gazarri's, doing the Watusi with Sam The Sham.
she's mainlining heroin in a cardboard box.

June Fairchild isn't dead—
I saw her tying one on at King Eddy's Saloon.
she's making *Drive, He Said,* with Jack Nicholson.
she's selling the *Daily News* in front of the courthouse.
she's snorting Ajax for the camera.

June Fairchild isn't dead—
she's relapsing in front of the Alexandria Hotel.
she's working as a taxi dancer, making $200 a shift.
I saw her vamping with Hefner, frugging on YouTube.
she's naming Danny Hutton's band "Three Dog Night."

June Fairchild isn't dead—
she's living at the Roslyn SRO on Main.
she's giving up her daughter to her ex.
she's snorting Ajax for the camera.
she's planning a comeback, needs new headshots.

June Fairchild isn't dead—
she's *Up In Smoke*, getting clean.
she's sitting by the phone.
she's falling asleep in Laurel Canyon
with a lit cigarette in her hand,
waiting for me to call.

Former Gazarri's dancer/starlet June Fairchild, a self-proclaimed "angel in a snake pit," died of liver cancer on February 17, 2015. She was 68 years old.

Tonight I Dream of My Last Meal with My First Ex-Husband, Who Was Both Fickle and Bent

There was yet another threesome on the menu. Him, the platinum divorcée from next door, and that TV actress who followed me home. A triple-decker: blonde on blonde on blonde. Hold the mayo. I knew they'd hit it off. Like replacement china. Each of them chipped someplace marginal. I admit to damaged, self-besotted, brunette. When I married him I thought: *I will divorce you in a year.* What was *he* thinking? He used to tie me to the bed posts—the only way he could get off. I didn't mind. He hated that. When the shenanigans paled, and his money ran out, *I* wanted out. Was that when he decided to keep me, *and* the TV actress, *and* the platinum blonde? Never could make up his mind. His dick (did I mention?) was slanted to the left, like his politics. A girl could get addicted to that bit of kink.

Tonight I Dream of My Second Ex-Husband,
Who Played Piano Better than Herbie Hand-Cock

Naked and unperturbed, hard-on the size of an Eagle Scout's flashlight, he watches me sleep, standing at my bedside like he still lives here. Framed drawings of me, seventeen and naked, hang like cautionary muses above my bed. His eyes devour them like that sweet girl still exists. Like he didn't grind her into extinction with each lie, each humiliating indiscretion. In this dream he's twenty-five, and almost sure he loves me. And then he's thirty. And then he's gone. But right now he's tonguing me from behind (that drawing of me on all fours), my labia symmetrical, curving against my inner thighs like geometry. He fingers his cock. He looks like Wesley Snipes in *Blade*. He pinches my left nipple, his practiced mouth seeking out my complicity. Why does the fantasy always best real life? My second ex-husband sits on the edge of my dream, smoothes the hair from my forehead with his piano-widened hands. When his fingers dance arpeggios on my face it feels like foreplay. When I reach for the dildo on the nightstand, it starts itself.

Out of Body

She puts bowls on the table,
fixates on the scarred oak union,
digs her resentment into the grooves.

This is how he knows her:

She yawls.
Drowns him
out.

He eats her temporal lobe. Skim milk splashes
in the bowl. 5% body fat;
a new low.

Riddle: When is a promise like a bayonet?

I've been meaning to tell you.
A woman betrayed in a breakfast nook does not
constitute a poem.

Her dead mother reaches through the wall,
throws the marriage in her face.

Her husband grabs his bowl and a spoon.

"Sit down, darling," he says.
"Open wide."

Because He Used to Love Her:
A Story in Photographs and Senryu

The train station. The ex-lover. The long-legged girl.

1

the duffle holds her
zipped-up life; girl on the run
silhouette of fear

high-strung, he called her
a colt in stilettos
bolting in the night

2   she played him, his heart on her finger, her broken vows…where was his ring?

3   was that his shadow?
skittish, she feared his revenge—
saw him everywhere

Enter Here | 72

4

her hair like a whip
torturing him now, but once
he did worship her

5

she slips out the gate
he spies a flash of sleekness
her colt legs fleeing

long drink of water
his thirst unquenchable, his
reach beyond the sea

Regarding the Unreliability of Buses in the Desert in Late July

—for Chelsea Kashergen

The Girl
She wouldn't last the afternoon.

Chalk white. Redheaded determination against
the soul-crushing Mohave.

What kind of life was it anyway,
when the closest thing to civilization was a mall
twenty miles away?

The pretty ones, her mama said,
rarely had far to walk.

The Mother
Nothing ages a woman like a dead kid.
Except, maybe, the desert.
Skin turned to parchment.
Age spots on her hands. *A penance.*

She stuffed them in her pockets.

The Man
The girl climbed into his dusty pickup.
Those tiny shorts, metal zipper flashing back
the sun, playing off the skin of her inner thigh.

It was like a dream, he told the police.

The Mall
glistened. Macy's. Target. The Body Shop. Mrs. Field's.
The Sharper Image.
Victoria's Secret. Wetzel's Pretzels.
Every Kiss Begins With Kay.

The Mother
She sat at the table in the small trailer and
watched the sun flatline behind the highway.
Then she raised her glass of hard lemonade.

Here's to the dead kid. She saluted
the faded snapshot, tacked up above the sink.

The blue-eyed girl in the photo
looked right through her.

Outside, the highway trembled as the bus
whizzed by, asphalt searing the tires,
their high whine a love song, a murmur.

My girl. The one with big ambition.
We all figured she'd be the one to get away.

For Lynnie in the Dark

She married him in Vegas.
She'd already paid for the chapel.
She did it to please her dying mom.

She fingered his photo in her pocket.
He gave her his adored mom's ruby ring.
She didn't know what synthetic meant.

She walked down the aisle in a panic.
He didn't tell her he'd always been an orphan.
She had forgotten her bouquet.

He liked aimless drives in the desert.
He liked how she mated his socks.
He kissed her senseless.

Their bedroom was an illusion.
He stepped into his pants like a fireman.
He was in cahoots with the Lord.

She had an Italian complexion.
She'd recently lost her keys.
He had exceptional footwork.

She sold her condo near the beach.
She sold all her Santa Fe-style furniture.
He allowed her to take both cats.

He paid for everything on her Visa.
He moved her to a small town in Utah.
He heard Ted Bundy was imprisoned nearby.

She got knee-deep into religion.
She got her real estate license.
He got a pink slip on Friday.

He blamed it on her and the meds.
He dreamed of red meat and hawks, circling.
She made more money than God.

She danced in his head like a migraine.
He had his second stepfather's temper.
She called Dial-A-Prayer, then hung up.

He followed the *tele-novellas*.
He was headed for a cliff when the car stalled.
She put Revlon concealer on her bruises.

He fell off the couch.
She was in L.A. when it hit her.
She opened a secret bank account and drove back to Utah.

He shot her the first time in the leg.
She didn't move.
He watched her not moving.

She remembered she forgot to feed the cats.
She curled up.
She squeezed her eyes shut.

He squeezed the trigger.
He squeezed it again.
She knew her dancing days were done.

He shot himself in the head.

—for Lynn Cutolo, murdered on October 3, 2007. RIP.

When the Handsome, Overgrown Samoan Boy Stands Again in Front of Your Glass-Walled Beach House in Venice & Begins to Masturbate, Never Taking His Eyes Off You...

Lock eyes with your accomplice.

This is what comes with glass houses.

He will touch himself through denim.
His dick will break free of his cut-off jeans,

Bigger than a cucumber.

Don't worry! His eyes will never leave your face.
No one will guess your truth.

Reach under your skirt, pull aside your panties,
Touch your rock hard clit.

Watch your reflection in the window glass as
Daylight shifts into dusk.

Look at his face as you make yourself come.

This is how you cope with loss.

I Was Hovering Just Below the Hospital Ceiling, Contemplating My Death

when I glanced down and saw my body,
the suffering, damaged girl.

My beloved, nowhere to be found,
had died on impact.

Now the ER doctors say I can go either way.

So I hover on the Sistine ceiling
of the ICU, undecided, my dead lover's
hand reaching for me
like God stretched for Adam.

The tubes and machines that keep me
earthbound give way.

We soar above the hospital morgue,
backtrack the highway, our bodies
unbroken, the crash spliced out.

My mother keens beside my hospital bed,
her fingers tangled in my blood-soaked hair,
picking at pieces of windshield.
Holding tight.

Years later I retrace the road
between death and Santa Barbara,
how he cradled my head in his lap as he drove.

How he didn't want to go with me.
How I always got what I wanted.

All my life, such a greedy girl.

Author's Commentary: When I was twenty, a highway collision killed my fiancé and my unborn child. I survived only because I was asleep, my head on my fiancé's lap, when the driver of the other vehicle veered into our lane and crashed into us at 70mph. I have tried for years to write about the immediate aftermath. This poem is the first time I got it right.

Five Ways I'm a Bad Girl

1. the players:

Cybil & her three Rottweilers join us at the beach. Sally comes with Dr. Diane who says if I need anything medical, she's my guy. That night me and Mickey are fucking, getting a little loud. Dr. Diane sniffs around, hang-dog, all *Jesus, mamasita. Make me howl like that.*

2. the complications:

Sally must have her on a short leash. Next night when the ocean spits sand in my cornea, Dr. Diane corners me in the john, just under the pulsing, overhead light, removes the culprit from my eye, tapes it shut with a white gauze patch.

3. resolve out the window:

She locks the door. Licks the beach salt from my face. *I heard you two last night. What's Mickey got, makes you yowl like a cat?* Oh, how did my legs become wrapped around her face, her pinpoint tongue ramming into me, slamming my ass against the sink?

4. the excuse:

I'm a sucker for sweet talk. A sycophant for sin. Half-blinded by the gauze patch. Born to give in.

5. the denouement:

Sally's outside the door. Mickey sleeps like a baby. Dr. Diane swears that after she's married, nothing between us will change. While Cybil walks the Rottweilers, I escape down the beach. Dr. Diane retreats to Sally's low self-esteem. They decide to go for Chinese. When Mickey awakens, nobody's home.

At Eighteen

When I wanted to be seen
When I danced out to the edge
When I was so afraid to love

When I longed to be a Marilyn
When I slept my way to the top
When I opened my legs but not my heart

When I shouted at my mother over dinner:
When I grow up I'll be somebody,
not like you.

When I took a lover twice my age
When I told him I wanted photos
wearing only my grandmother's

ruby necklace
When he shot me, butt-naked
on my mother's oriental rug

When I went home to flaunt the affair
When I fluttered a cache of the photos
onto her bed

When she walked to her closet and opened
the bottom drawer
When she handed me a large, blue envelope

When I looked at photos of my mother, naked,
her young face wicked, movie-star dreamy
When I recognized the girl who wore only a ruby necklace

and looked like she had plans even bigger than mine

When she said, *I was only sixteen. He was forty.*

Red-Handed in Canoga Park:
How Everything Is All My Fault

We were five, and three. I had just learned how to ride. You sat behind me on my blue bike, hung on tightly the four blocks to the drugstore. They had toys. Paddle Ball, jacks, stuffed animals. I was entranced by the My Merry kitchen set. Thumb-sized boxes of Ivory Snow, Kleenex, Ajax, and my favorite, a perfect replica bottle of Windex. The stuff of my dollhouse dreams. The restraint I had exhibited on previous visits failed me. I jabbed my finger through the cellophane, that tiny, blue bottle irresistible. You palmed the tiny Chlorox, reached for the Brillo pads. "Hey!" the manager shouted, his bigness looming down the aisle. There was no place to hide. When I ran, you froze. When I got on my bike and sped off, you faced the music. This day has defined our sisterhood. I was five for Pete's sake. Forgive me.

Morning Wood

"Touch it," he says.

My lips graze the tip.

His penis tastes
like sleep.

In his
hips'
hollow,

between
his pincer
thighs, I nestle.

Open-windowed
sunlight
climbs the walls,

honeys his dear
face.

I long to inhabit him.

"Do you think
of your penis

as an 'It'
or a 'He'?"

"Neither," he says.
"I think of it as 'Me.'"

Housekeeping

Ashs to ashes, dust to Swiffer.

I love you like a cat loves an ankle,
rubbed up against, territorial.

I love you like the Swiffer loves
the dust, deeply, with an
electrostatic charge.

When you're gone
I shout your name.
I match your socks.
I scrub the kitchen sink.

Am I not your beloved?

Hidden in a heap of laundry,
I touch myself,
come on your warm, white
sheets.

If you see a trail of glistening
girl sparkling across your coverlet,
know it as a road map to me.

Tonight We Will Bloom for One Night Only

Tonight you must plow me a respite between the moonflowers,
mock orange, night phlox, and *Epiphyllum Oxypetalum.*
You must open me to the summer night like cereus.

You must pick my perversions like petals, allow them
for one night to bloom, frangipani wafting, a concupiscent
wind humming at my door.

I've surrendered to your heady sweat of primrose, plumeria,
addicted to your outstretched arms of night-blooming jasmine,
my heliotrope buds hard and wanting, reeking of Madagascar vanilla
with its accompanying moral ambiguity.

I am more than a day lily.

We are each bodies, hard-wired for pleasure,
destined for momentary blooming,
then extinction.

When the bats swarm and the moths sidle up to this one night
of fevered pollination, let's be ready.

Let's face them, our appetency the headlights
they slam into again and again.

We will make our escape at first light. Singing.

Roman Holiday

Pino has the tiniest dick in Europe.
My sister's thumb and forefinger
are a scant inch apart.

When it comes
to postmortems, she's worse than a man.

We stroll Villa Borghese like lovers.
The air reeks of jasmine.
We have just viewed the Caravaggios,
and are drunk on art and our own power.

This summer we've been screwing
our way through Europe,
a Brit, a Dane, two Spaniards, an Austrian
record producer, and a set of tri-lingual
Croatian twins.

Even the Texans we hooked up with near the
Spanish Steps stood no chance.

The tall blond boy & my sister, getting
sexy in the back of the restaurant;
me & the dark one, reckless,
his thick hand on my thigh.

Next week we'll move on to the Florentines
(lecherous, slick) and we will treat more men badly,
one city as good as another,
cutting a swath of calculated payback for
every man who ever broke our hearts.

When you're this beautiful, my sister says,
it's always a race against time.

I Prefer Pussy (a little city-kitty ditty)

I prefer pussy, as in cat
as in willow
as in chases a rat
as in raised on a pillow.

I prefer pussy, as in riot
as in foots
as in pussycat doll
as in puss-in-boots.

I prefer pussy, as a twat
it is not, nor
is it a beaver,
a clam or a cleaver.

I prefer pussy to
nookie or gash;
it isn't a box,
or a cave or a slash.

I prefer pussy to snapper
or snatch, far better
than taco or
slit or man-catch.

I prefer pussy, though
rosebud's not bad,
and muffin sounds homey,
and cooch makes me glad.

I prefer pussy, as in whip
as in flower
as into it you slip—
as in *I* have the power.

Cousin Elaine from Chicago and I Are Naked

In the space between taking off our clothes
and putting on our swimsuits,

we stand naked.
My chest is flat as a board.

Her curves are already legendary,
her breasts bursting from her bikini.

I want to run my fingers along
their goose-bumped perimeter,
lick their chocolate tips.

I am 12 and shouldn't think this way.

I shouldn't think about her tanned legs
thrown over mine on the couch,
nights when we watch TV, shouldn't

think about the damp between my thighs
when she bunks with me at night,

when dreams of following her back to Chicago
consume my sleep.

In the pool, she's a silver fish;
my body's a heat-seeking missile.

"Marco!" she calls from the deep end,
her eyes shut tight.

"Polo!" I whisper in her shell ear.
When I reach for her she does not pull away.

When she kisses me, open-mouthed, I pull
the string on her bikini, free her breasts,
bury my lips between them.

When I speak of this day in our far-off future,
she'll say it never happened, swear it was all a dream.

Dear Mrs. Brown, Your Husband Whimpers
When He Comes

1.

"I want my wife to know all about us," he says. We're close together on the couch, but not yet touching. She needn't worry. "What is there to know? Just tell her I don't fuck married men." I see his sad face crumble. Mr. Brown hates the truth almost as much as he hates bad language. Sometimes I curse to rile him but tonight it just comes out. We're back from dinner at Miceli's on Melrose, that lonely table in the back in the dark and so far from San Pedro no one he knows will find him. I suddenly want more out of life.

Mr. Brown pulls me to him. His tweed sports coat scratches my bare arms. I breathe in his Amphora pipe tobacco and English Leather. He smells like my dad, who never held me like this. Unused to kissing, Mr. Brown's tentative lips brush mine. I push my tongue past his teeth. His erection, a pup tent of unrequited love. Against my better judgement, I let him dry hump my thigh.

Afterward, I fix my hair at the hallway mirror while Mr. Brown fastens a locket around my neck. I can make out an "L" in bright diamonds. It is not my initial. "L?" My eyes catch his in the reflection. "For Lust," he smiles. (Or maybe L for his wife, Lucia, or L for Leaving her, I don't say.) L for Lonely. Looney. *Lost,* I think as Mr. Brown's hands roam my body, the shiny locket the price of admission. I stare at our mismatched reflections, the almost incestuous nature of our non-romance. I finger the Jaeger-Lecoultre Reverso watch he gave me last fall (that rough patch when he left his wife for all of a week until she threatened suicide, again.) Mr. Brown showed me the texts. Before he went home, he gave me Lucia's watch. "She'll never miss it," he said as he fastened it on my wrist. She has excellent taste.

2.

When I visit Mr. Brown's bedside after the quadruple bypass, I put the extravagant blue-iris bouquet in a vase, perch on his hospital bed, and fill him in about my fucked-up life, the flood in the kitchen, my crappy new boss. He complains about the hospital food and remarks how a heart attack can truly mess up your day. I confess how lonely I am without him. "I'm thinking of leaving my wife," he tells me. I let him feel me up. "My heart attack is a wake-up call," he says. "*Carpe Diem.*"

On a hunch, I ask him when he's buying the red Corvette. "Blue," Mr. Brown says. "I ordered it in blue." Like the irises. Like the hospital walls. "Like the way I am without you," I admit. I'm about to ask him to take me along to pick up the new wheels, when Lucia and her friends waltz into the room. They see him, all over me, on his bed, her lost locket around my neck, her fancy watch on my wrist; Mrs. Brown's face darkens. Her friends gather her close, circle the wagons until I depart. Out of the corner of my eye I see her grab the blue irises from their vase, hurl them across the room.

3.

By the time I find out, Mr. Brown has been dead a year. I haven't seen him in a decade. I was not going to put out; he would not divorce Lucia. I never did ride in that blue Corvette. Soon I found myself a French photographer with a large dick and no wedding ring. I don't know if Mr. Brown ever found anyone. His obituary read, *Stand-up guy, great husband, dad. Married sixty-six years. Pillar of the community. Charitable. A churchgoer.* He once swore to me I was his church.

I have the offerings to prove it.

Last Dance in NoHo

After that last sad fuck
we go dancing in NoHo.

Elena's a hot, typecast Latina.
Moves to anything with a beat.

Has a thing for Gloria Estefan.
I can never keep up.

A problem we treat with mescal
and osculation.

Turn off that big brain, she sez
when I won't get up from the bar.

But confusion tangles my feet.

Now even the sex is bad.
I decide to break up with her first.

Before you, I say, *I had a black man*
with a Porsche and a cock
the size of Acapulco.

He'd bend me over the hood and
fuck me with the engine running.

Elena pulls me onto the dance floor
one last time.

A smack works as well as
a twirl, girl. One fist whistles
past my face.

Before you, she says, *I had this Asian girl.*
She didn't disrespect me.
She didn't talk back.

She fucking knew how to dance.

Daylight Savings Won't Save Us

If I pull the drapes it is always night.

I cannot see the seasons,
or you, sneaking off in the half-light
like there's someplace you'd rather be.

Come Monday, it will grow cold and dark
before people leave work.

Maybe you should go with them?

When I photograph you,
I stash my feelings in my pocket
where you won't find them,
where the fabric sticks to my
thighs.

Go downtown, you'd whisper, back
when it mattered, push my face
into your sunlit forever.

Can I help it if we are now on different clocks?

A hot pink August has stumbled
into our November like a second chance.
Why can't you see it?

Come Sunday, the saving of daylight
will no longer matter.
If I photograph the light, maybe you
will no longer matter.

I grab my camera and shoot the dawn
from the roof of our building.
Catch you slipping out the lobby.

My world goes dark without you.

Snow White: For Desirée, Former Headliner at 4Play Gentlemen's Club

I'd have worshipped you if you'd have let me.

I'd have swept you up in a Disney film, waltzed you
till the dwarves trudged home to their disenchanted wives,
whistled while you worked
the pole.

I wanted to detach your feet
from their stilettos, spirit you
from the stage, massage
your toes.

I wanted to wipe the hurt from your face,
and your arms, and your memory—
every queen's curse that led you here,
every charming prince
who let you down.

I wanted to wake you from the spell
of easy money, extricate you
from the donsie cluster of regulars,
those solitary gnomes who stuffed
twenties in your panties
who said you were the fairest in the land.

I'd have spirited you from this sleazy
skin palace, past L.A.'s concrete forest,
ensconced you in my feather bed,
released you from your glass-coffin future.

I wanted to save you, to savor
the taste of redemption on your lips,

sweet, like bluebirds,
like a fresh start.

Oh! Snow White!
Why couldn't you just be grateful?
Instead, the mirror on the wall reflected
your indifference.

When you left I plastered
your photo on the stage door of every
strip joint in L.A.

You: tousled, sun-kissed, clothed
for once, and reaching
for the poison apple.

Me: doing nothing to stop you.

For Kate in Absentia

Your husband has fallen in love.
He says she's a lot like you. A painter
he met in a bar. They danced all night.

Just like the two of you, at that dive bar
in Santa Fe (when you called at 3 a.m. to say
you'd finally met someone).

When he came to visit, your husband
stayed here. His new love lives close by.
He returned from her arms, all sparkly, school-
boy giddy. Not like last year,

when he was walking wounded, watching
his cell-phone video of your forest burial,
over and over (the one I still can't get
out of my head).

Your husband has fallen in love. But
she's married and her spouse is abusive, although
he's "never touched her." *She's ready
to leave him,* your husband says.

I tell him abut our friend, Lynnie,
whose husband "never touched her" either,
until she tried to leave and he shot her
twice in the head.

And there's your voice in my ear, Kate.
Watch out for my husband, you whisper.
He's always been naïve.

—for Kate O'Donnell

this small rain

this small rain sambas on San Vicente
wanders through Whittier
mambos past Montebello
and East L.A.

this small rain moves like a Latina
over-plucks her eyebrows
drinks tequila shooters
fronts a girl-band

this small rain works two jobs
dawdles in down-pours
this small rain seeds clouds

this small rain drives to Vegas in a *tormenta*
has a friend in Jesus
needs boots and a winter coat

in this drought-wracked city,
this small rain dreams of flash floods,
depósitos, indigo lakes,
cisterns, high water,
Big Gulps, endless refills

in this drought-wracked city,
this small rain settles on the *hierba seca*
sleeps under freeways
plays the lotto
is unlucky in love

this small rain longs to hose down the highways
this small rain chases storms

this small rain has a tsunami in her heart

this small rain kamikazes
in the gutter
suicides on summer sidewalks
dreams of a deluge
that overflows the river banks
washes L.A. clean

in this drought-wracked city,
this small rain scans the heavens,
looking for a monsoon,
searching for *su salvador*
in the reclaimed desert sky.

---

1. *tormenta:* rainstorm
2. *depósitos:* reservoirs
3. *hierba seca:* dry grass
4. *su salvador:* her savoir

Enter Here | 102

Acknowledgments: Photographs

All photographs shot and copyrighted by Alexis Rhone Fancher. All rights reserved. Photographs reproduced herein by permission.

- Cover: Downtown Los Angeles (DTLA), woman entering door on Seventh Street, July 2015
- Page 16: DTLA, turnstiles at Pershing Square Metro Station, June 2015
- Page 36: DTLA, Seventh Street parking lot, December 2013
- Page 49: DTLA, 212 West Sixth Street, mural by unknown artist which unfortunately was painted over in November 2016
- Page 58: DTLA, Artisan House, man with tattooed neck, 2015
- Page 65: June Fairchild's signature and telephone number which she wrote on a napkin for the author, 2014
- Pages 69–73: Five photographs of "Ann at the Train Station," summer 2015
- Page 97: Mary Fae Smith with Snow White mural, Venice Beach Boardwalk, 2013
- Page 102: DTLA, woman in Pershing Square Park, December 2015
- Page 111: Self-Portrait of the Author, 2016

Acknowledgments:
Previous Publications by Title of Poem

- Bambi Explains It All | *Carbon Culture Review*
- Because He Used to Love Her: A Story in Photographs and Senryu | *KYSO Flash*
- Boy Toy (Learning to Share) | *Hobart*
- Cousin Elaine and I Are Naked | *Fjords Review*
- Daddy's Friend, Stan | *Quaint Magazine*, **which nominated this poem for the 2015 Best of the Net Anthology**
- Daylight Savings Won't Save Us | *Gyroscope Review*
- Doggy-Style Christmas | *W.I.S.H.* (Walking Is Still Honest Press), in "Mistletoe Manifesto"
- Double Date: The Quarterback, the Fullback, & the High Cost of Dinner | *Tinderbox Poetry Journal*
- Family Tree | *Rat's Ass Review*
- Five Ways I'm a Bad Girl | *Rat's Ass Review*
- For Kate in Absentia | *Nashville Review*
- For the Sad Waitress at the Diner in Barstow | *San Pedro River Review*
- Freeway Sex | *Ragazine*
- Housekeeping | *Loch Raven Review*
- I Prefer Pussy (a little city-kitty ditty) | *KYSO Flash*
- I Was Hovering Just Below the Hospital Ceiling, Contemplating My Death | poem and commentary first published in *Glass: A Journal of Poetry*
- June Fairchild isn't dead— | *Cleaver Magazine*
- Larceny: A Story in Eleven Parts | *Scissors & Spackle;* and *Phantom Billstickers Café Reader* (New Zealand)
- Last Dance in NoHo | *Rat's Ass Review*
- Morning Wood | *KYSO Flash*

- Norwegian Wood | *streetcake magazine* (Issue 46) [poem previously published as "Murakami Cento Love Poem #1"]
- Out of Body | *Kleft Jaw*
- Play It As It Lays | *Mead: The Magazine of Literature and Libations*
- Red-Handed in Canoga Park: How Everything Is All My Fault | Silver Birch Press *Learning to Ride Anthology*
- Regarding the Unreliability of Buses in the Desert in Late July | *Loch Raven Review*
- Roman Holiday | *San Diego Poetry Annual 2017;* and *Serving House Journal* (Kowit's Korner) **[awarded Honorable Mention in the first Steve Kowit Poetry Prize competition (2016)]**
- Spreading My Legs for Someone (Posing for Pirelli) | *Thirteen Myna Birds*
- Stiletto Killer | *Thirteen Myna Birds*
- Tattooed Girl in a Sheer, White Blouse (Sushi Bar Fantasy) | *Chiron Review*
- Tattooed Girl on the Roof of King Eddy's Saloon with a Run in Her Last Pair of Stockings | *Slipstream* (Issue 25), **which nominated this poem for a Pushcart Prize**
- Tattooed Girl: Slice/Shokunin | *Chiron Review*
- the cool wind comes through me like Jamaica | *Ragazine*
- this small rain | *Kind of a Hurricane Press* **[awarded Honorable Mention in Editor's Poetry Contest 2014]**; also anthologized in *The Absence of Something Specified* (Fern Rock Falls Press, 2016); **and nominated for a Pushcart Prize by a Pushcart Contributing Editor**
- Three Little Words | *Cactus Heart*
- To my new boyfriend with blue lips tattooed on his neck | *Anti-Heroin Chic*

- Tonight I Dream of Anjelica, My First Ex-Girlfriend, Who Taught Me the Rules of the Road... | *Pittsburgh Poetry Review*
- Tonight I Dream of My First True Love (*Ménage à Trois*) | *Hobart*
- Tonight I Dream of My Last Meal with My First Ex-Husband Who Was Both Fickle and Bent | *Menacing Hedge*
- Tonight I Dream of My Second Ex-Husband Who Played Piano Better than Herbie Hand-Cock | *Menacing Hedge*
- Tonight We Will Bloom for One Night Only | **First-Prize Winner, Los Angeles Poets Society Summer Contest (2014)**
- Tuesday Nights, Room 28 of the Royal Motel on Little Santa Monica | *Little Raven Four* [anthology]
- When I turned fourteen, my mother's sister took me to lunch and said: | *Ragazine* **[also chosen by Edward Hirsch for inclusion in *The Best American Poetry 2016*]**
- When I turned sixteen, Mother let Uncle Kenny from Chicago take me for a ride | *Alyss*
- When the Handsome, Overgrown Samoan Boy Stands Again in Front of Your Glass-Walled Beach House in Venice & Begins to Masturbate, Never Taking His Eyes Off You... | *Scissors & Spackle*
- When your mother convinces you to take in your homeless younger sister | *Ragazine*
- Years & Years Later I Am Still Not That Girl, Laughing | *Askew*

Acknowledgments:
Previous Publications by Title of Venue

- *Alyss* | When I turned sixteen, Mother let Uncle Kenny from Chicago take me for a ride
- *Anti-Heroin Chic* | To my new boyfriend with blue lips tattooed on his neck
- *Askew* | Years & Years Later I Am Still Not That Girl, Laughing
- *Cactus Heart* | Three Little Words
- *Carbon Culture Review* | Bambi Explains It All
- *Chiron Review* | Tattooed Girl in a Sheer, White Blouse (Sushi Bar Fantasy)
- *Chiron Review* | Tattooed Girl: Slice/Shokunin
- *Cleaver Magazine* | June Fairchild isn't dead
- *Fjords Review* | Cousin Elaine and I Are Naked
- *Glass: A Journal of Poetry* | I Was Hovering Just Below the Hospital Ceiling, Contemplating My Death [plus commentary]
- *Gyroscope Review* | Daylight Savings Won't Save Us
- *Hobart* | Boy Toy (Learning to Share)
- *Hobart* | Tonight I Dream of My First True Love (*Ménage à Trois*)
- **Kind of a Hurricane Press, Editor's Poetry Contest 2014, Honorable Mention** | this small rain [also anthologized in *The Absence of Something Specified* (Fern Rock Falls Press, 2016); **and nominated by a Pushcart Contributing Editor for a Pushcart Prize**]
- *Kleft Jaw* | Out of Body
- *KYSO Flash* | Because He Used to Love Her: A Story in Photographs and Senryu
- *KYSO Flash* | I Prefer Pussy (a little city-kitty ditty)
- *KYSO Flash* | Morning Wood

- *Little Raven Four* [anthology] | Tuesday Nights, Room 28 of the Royal Motel on Little Santa Monica
- *Loch Raven Review* | Housekeeping
- *Loch Raven Review* | Regarding the Unreliability of Buses in the Desert in Late July
- **Los Angeles Poets Society Summer Contest (2014), First-Prize Winner** | Tonight We Will Bloom for One Night Only
- *Mead: The Magazine of Literature and Libations* | Play It As It Lays [previously published as "Play It As It Lays Poem #2"]
- *Menacing Hedge* | Tonight I Dream of My Last Meal with My First Ex-Husband Who Was Both Fickle and Bent
- *Menacing Hedge* | Tonight I Dream of My Second Ex-Husband Who Played Piano Better than Herbie Hand-Cock
- *Nashville Review* | For Kate in Absentia
- *Phantom Billstickers Café Reader* (New Zealand) | Larceny: A Story in Eleven Parts
- *Pittsburgh Poetry Review* | Tonight I Dream of Anjelica, My First Ex-Girlfriend, Who Taught Me the Rules of the Road…
- *Quaint Magazine,* **which nominated this poem for the 2015 Best of the Net Awards and Anthology** | Daddy's Friend, Stan
- *Ragazine* | Freeway Sex
- *Ragazine* | the cool wind comes through me like Jamaica
- *Ragazine* | When I turned fourteen, my mother's sister took me to lunch and said: **[also chosen by Edward Hirsch for inclusion in *The Best American Poetry 2016*]**
- *Ragazine* | When your mother convinces you to take in your homeless younger sister
- *Rat's Ass Review* | Family Tree
- *Rat's Ass Review* | Five Ways I'm a Bad Girl
- *Rat's Ass Review* | Last Dance in NoHo

- *San Diego Poetry Annual 2017* | Roman Holiday **[awarded Honorable Mention in the first Steve Kowit Poetry Prize competition (2016)]**
- *San Pedro River Review* | For the Sad Waitress at the Diner in Barstow
- *Scissors & Spackle* | Larceny: A Story in Eleven Parts
- *Scissors & Spackle* | When the Handsome, Overgrown Samoan Boy Stands Again in Front of Your Glass-Walled Beach House in Venice & Begins to Masturbate, Never Taking His Eyes Off You...
- *Serving House Journal* (Kowit's Korner) | Roman Holiday **[awarded Honorable Mention in the first Steve Kowit Poetry Prize competition (2016)]**
- Silver Birch Press *Learning to Ride Anthology* | Red-Handed in Canoga Park: How Everything Is All My Fault
- *Slipstream* (Issue 25), **which nominated this poem for a Pushcart Prize** | Tattooed Girl on the Roof of King Eddy's Saloon with a Run in Her Last Pair of Stockings
- *streetcake magazine* (Issue 46) | Norwegian Wood [poem previously published as "Murakami Cento Love Poem #1"]
- *The Absence of Something Specified* (Fern Rock Falls Press, 2016) | this small rain **[awarded Honorable Mention in Editor's Poetry Contest 2014, Kind of a Hurricane Press; and nominated for a Pushcart Prize by a Pushcart Contributing Editor]**
- *Thirteen Myna Birds* | Spreading My Legs for Someone (Posing for Pirelli)
- *Thirteen Myna Birds* | Stiletto Killer
- *Tinderbox Poetry Journal* | Double Date: The Quarterback, the Fullback, & the High Cost of Dinner
- *W.I.S.H.* (Walking Is Still Honest Press), in "Mistletoe Manifesto" | Doggy-Style Christmas

Author's Bio

Alexis Rhone Fancher is the author of *How I Lost My Virginity To Michael Cohen and other heart-stab poems* (Sybaritic Press, 2014) and *State of Grace: The Joshua Elegies* (KYSO Flash Press, 2015).

Her poems appear in more than 100 literary magazines, journals, and anthologies, including *The Best American Poetry 2016, Wide Awake: Poets of Los Angeles and Beyond, Rattle, The MacGuffin, Slipstream, Hobart, Cleaver Magazine, Poetry East, Fjords Review, Rust + Moth, Plume, Tinderbox Poetry Journal, Askew,* and *Nashville Review*; and her photographs have been published worldwide, including spreads in *River Styx, Heart Online,* and *Rogue Agent,* and on the covers of *Heyday Magazine, Chiron Review, Witness,* and *The Mas Tequila Review*. Her writing has been nominated multiple times for the Pushcart Prize and Best of the Net.

A lifelong Angeleno, Alexis is poetry editor of *Cultural Weekly,* where she also publishes a monthly photo-essay, "The Poet's Eye," about her on-going love affair with Los Angeles. From the S-curves of Topanga and the sprawling beaches of the Westside, to the stunning views of downtown L.A. from her 8th-floor loft studio, her beloved city can be construed as another character in her work.

Find out more at: www.alexisrhonefancher.com

Self-Portrait of the Author, 2016

"I write about women like me, women who own their sexuality and take responsibility for their choices. It may seem I'm writing about sex, but really, I'm writing about power. Who has it. How to get it. How to wield it. How to keep it."

—from "Featured Fem" Alexis Rhone Fancher, interviewed by The Fem *literary magazine (17 June 2016)*

Author's Note

Thank you to Cynthia Atkins, Francesca Bell, Michelle Bitting, Chanel Brenner, Tresha Haefner-Rubinstein, Ellaraine Lockie, and Tony Magistrale, for your ongoing wisdom, editing prowess, and high standards. Thank you to my publisher, Clare MacQueen. It is a joy to create with you. I am grateful to the city of Los Angeles for inspiring many of these poems. And thank you to my beloved Fancher, who knows me so well, and loves me still.

—Alexis Rhone Fancher
(*March, 2017*)

CPSIA information can be obtained
at www.ICGtesting.com
Printed in the USA
BVOW05s0826130517
484069BV00025B/487/P